MW00915012

The Phoenix and the Lotus

Todd Erick Pedersen

PRELUDE
The Radiant Dawn

"Tell me a story." Said the shining arc of the One, to the last radiant dawn....

"Sing me a song." Said then the freedom of the stars, to the cool blue of the Earth....

And, "Ask me a riddle." Said finally the white light of the moon, to the ceaselessness of the sea....

"Weave in the dream of the world, withal the meaning of love, and the Ever-Quest, for the still small voice in the wind, which is the whispering Spirit of God...."

BOOK I
Metaxaeus and Akasha

Metaxaeus at last began to look up. To glance up from his long orison, his lengthy space of meditation while sitting down beside the old well, He looked upwards for the first time that morning and as it were directly into the sun's uplifting light, its first tilting rays. As though tranquilly meeting its gaze, He then looked away into the changing skies further off in the distance: the mighty sheets of rain just a little ways away. But for now there were only those first rays of morning sunshine, just spilling over the lips of the distant mountains, like a kind of fine wine, to flood the land. There the spreading, emergent rays of daylight tilting over the whole countryside like some bright illumination to be bestowed upon the waiting world. For Metaxaeus, this morning already felt different, different to him from other mornings in which he kept the same routine as today: for this particular morning he felt within himself a strong premonition, causing him to tremble for a moment, that the things which he had grown used to would soon be changing for him, and changing in every way. He was a youth who would swear that he had already learned much, much about the land, the village, the country, and the people whom he had walked amongst ever since the early days of his childhood. But also, and more importantly to him in his heart, he had learned much about a certain natural state of quietude within: indeed, had even heard once from a wise person a specific name given to this particular state of quietude, though he could not now think of what it had been.

So today, as every day, Metaxaeus had spent his morning there, pre-dawn, sitting down beside the well, and proceeding quietly and conscientiously with a sort of peaceful descent into himself, and thus learning from the fountain there. There drinking in his own illumination. Because for Metaxaeus, meditation had, even in the days of his early youth, already become a cultivated way of life.

So what kinds of things had he learned, then, aside from this state of quietude, and at such a young age, from this inward fountain of life?

Above all he had learned a kind of wakened dreaming, crisp in its always arising, undaunted ceaseless flow. Though also he had learned that beneath the flow lies a perfectly still center, not unlike that of a rose or a lotus: a sleeplessly unfolding and yet still-centered flow, like a river and its source, or an almighty rush that is ever irrupting from the timeless moment. And he had learned that this wakened dreaming had to it a kind of tendency towards the world, a tendency that, he thought, seemed to be to merge with the world around him, to merge in coincidence and a kind of serendipity.

From sitting daily down beside the well, Metaxaeus had learned all this. In the early hours before dawn and sitting silently and conscientiously alone with himself, he had learned at an early age whatever there was that he now realized about life.

Beginning to grow uncomfortable at the sight of the gathering clouds, the thunderheads forming along the horizon, Metaxaeus at last stood up from his morning orison and began to walk in the direction of his home in the village. Occupying his thoughts as he went was the question of how to fulfill his plan to leave from his village without disappointing his father and mother, as well as the problem of how he was going to find the work that he would need in order to gain a living.

He knew himself to be one who lived in his dreaming: a young man who spent the watch of his afternoons and his evenings, and oft even his midnights, attuned to the dreams continually roiling their way into and through his thoughts, and teeming within his psyche. The one thing he knew that he could do, though, if given the chance, the one doubtless ability that he had in his possession, was to work wonders with stone. For he could see an image, or often even a train of images, in his mind's eye, and could then take that image and realize its shape faultlessly into a piece of stone.

He knew neither how to read nor write. Nevertheless he thought that if he could find a way to use his handiwork to show to the world, or at least to those nearest and dearest to his heart, the inmost workings of his soul, that then perhaps he might even become famous for his art, the curiously bespoken truth into stone.

Again, this is what he knew how to do: he knew how to take from that fountain within and to soak up its knowledge and then how to communicate this truth through the medium of sculpting stone. But where would he go? Without having had an opportunity to prove himself, how could he convince the master stoneworkers abroad to let him demonstrate his talents to them?

He had with him a hope.

In his pocket he carried a miniature of what had long been his favorite image to sculpt, and which had long been the image that most pressed itself to the fore of his imagination, the elegant combination of two strange yet powerful symbols, each taken separately but then fashioned into one, into a kind of synthesis that for some odd reason had most endured through the fire of his dreams, and remained at the forefront of his vision.

What he held, then, was a tiny figurine no larger than that it could rest easily in the palm of one's hand, and if in its raw materials it might have an exorbitant monetary value, its real worth was in its masterful execution as a truly pristine work of art. One might even have surmised that only the most mature artist could have wrought this small miracle in stone. For Metaxaeus had somehow managed to flawlessly combine a cut of sapphire with a piece of alabaster. But the artistic feat was that he had also sculpted both, and then fastened them inextricably together: a sapphire top rising seamlessly up from an alabaster base. The other mystery of how he came to have in his possession the twin substances of both sapphire and alabaster, and each in just the precise quantity that he could have molded from them this miniature figurine, was a secret that he guarded as closely as those dreams themselves, of his, through which this was wrought.

Now, the base he had carved into the liveliest and most lifelike pattern of a lotus blossom, so that you would swear that you saw there not stone, but leaves, verily a flower that might well rustle in the breeze, while the top, emergent from the base, had been fashioned into the feathery fiery likeness of a bird that he had continually heard about in tales growing up as a boy, and which had long since come to occupy the paramount place in that flowing river of images that made up his daily mind. He had had to visualize the blue fire, and then carve perfect in its realization this sapphirine phoenix, rare and mystical bird, rising up from the lotus blossom.

Yet for some strange reason the very idea of revealing this feat of his to others caused the inside of his chest, around the region of his heart, to flutter so much that he swore to himself that he would be the one to burst into a blue, consuming fire if this treasured statuette were ever to meet with any form of disdain or chagrin. Metaxaeus simply could not bear to have his heart-center, as it were, the very core of his youthful being, stepped upon by a master only envious of his skill, so for a season he would only continue to wonder.

What could he present to the stoneworkers in the capital city, that would prove to them his skill, yet at the same time not give away the all with which he was blessed?

In a different town far away from the village of Metaxaeus, a young girl, Akasha, spins her tales. Like the most skilled weaver, she has a gift for storytelling that is as preternatural in the world as anyone's gift for doing anything, as anybody's gift for doing anything at all.

For the tales she tells cause even the most wizened of hearts to belong to her as she unfolds her breathless stories. Young and old alike smile and laugh and weep and finally joy at the spirit and romance of these on-spinning motifs of love and trials and perseverance and even the ways of God and now and then ultimately even the ways of the greatest mystery of all, that of the source of creation itself. See in her thought, then, in her speech, and in her stories, questions encircling questions, and riddles answering to riddles. Akasha is gifted like none other.

The question arises, then, in the minds of her hearers, whence always this fountain of inner peace and wisdom and joy and creativity arising from the soul of such a youngster, and one apparently virgin in the ways of the world? The almighty taleteller-girl Akasha has, in her town and its environs, gotten to be quite the spectacle. Yet what of her own mind?

In one of her most popular stories she spins the tale of a youth with gifted hands who can sculpt any image from any stone, but who cannot figure out how to leave from his home. In this story told by Akasha endings vary and at times the boy makes his fortune and lives happily, in love with a girl from a distant city, but at others it ends badly and the boy at the last finds himself both broke and heartbroken, alone and darkly arthritic, bereft of the great and wonderful gift of his holy craft.

Let us not forget, however, that Akasha, away down in her heart, knows more than we do: and perhaps that is why in her thoughts she sometimes dreams of meeting just this youth sculptor wandered away from his very distant village, and his very distant home.

Inside his heart of hearts, Metaxaeus harbors his doubts about the world, and its people. Harbors his hopes, too. Everywhere (and with the eyes of a youth) he sees potential, but everywhere, too, he sees greed and hatred and lusts: the lust for power and the lust for material gain and all of the other lusts ever for the transient things of the world. He looks on with oft sad eyes for the window through which love must come through, and also wonders to himself, Whence always this bright invisibility, this strange and sifting inner light? This still fountain that I have found within myself, with its theatre of dreams. Do others know of this? For now, however, he must ask himself over and over again, as he day by day continues to grow and to reflect and to become supple in both body and mind, the questions, What is this blue, consuming fire at the center of my dreams? What am I? And what is to be my purpose?

BOOK II
The Soul of the World

Akasha awakes. Rises from bed; greets the day. Finishes her morning chores, and begins listening for the music, the music within, the music generally escaping her way, at this selfsame hour of the day. Her own orison of play....

She had once been up and away into the mountains, this when she was still but just a little girl. Lost for a moment, she bumped into a strange looking elderly man who claimed to be a magician. When he smiled at her, her feeling of uneasiness vanished, and she found she could not help but smile, too. He is the one who first talked to Akasha about the mystery of spirit, but up until a certain age she had always considered it far more important the moment when he touched with his hand her forehead, for that is when she felt dizzy for a minute, and afterwards when the feeling she always carried inside of her when telling her stories, began.

Now in the mornings and sitting still awaiting the music that comes floating its way into her room, into her heart, into her mind, she thinks often of that afternoon when she encountered the magician. Strange man. Strange things to say to one so young. What did he know? He spoke of the spirit as invisible, as everywhere, as continually aware of everything and everyone, including itself, and he spoke of its connection to the Maker of the World, and to each one of us. He laughed, then, and went on to say only that if you wanted to be in its presence, you would have to learn to sit very still, and to go all the way within yourself. This all he did say, and then he winked slyly and right at that moment must have handed to her a token, pressed into her open palm, although she was not aware of it at the moment that it happened. All she knew was that when she looked down at her hand she held in it a tiny figurine, and when she looked up again the old man was nowhere to be seen. As far as she could tell, the thing he had presumably pressed into the palm of her hand was nothing but the tiny statue of a boy, a boy who himself held something out in the palm of his own hand, but what it was, was far too small to make out. Since then, though, she had always kept the tiny statue in a place special to her, and that where no one else would be likely to find it. Until one day she realized that it had become precious to her, and she even imagined that when she was feeling cloudy or distressed, she could take up into her hands this trinket and begin to recover her calm or her clarity. She was beginning to get very superstitious.

Yet she continued to sit out her orison every morning, still and quiet, ever since that day of her girlhood, wondering each and every morning what the old man could have meant by those strange words about the spirit and its link to the Maker of the World. But by now she had learned to plunge deep into herself, and she saw things there, things she imagined that other people did not see. Also it was there, in that place of silence within herself, that dwelt the feeling she had when telling her stories, which she felt she had now learned, through practice, to be able to drop into whenever she willed.

At first, many people poked fun at her stories, and they were even discouraged by her older siblings and cousins and her parents, too. (Her grandparents, however, thought them to be delightful from the first.) But then, as she persisted and continued to tell her stories to others, gradually they began to grow into a marvel, and she would often include in them, unbeknownst to her, details of the lives of the people who would be listening. And this was too much: this seeming ability on behalf of a child to peer into the daily lives, as if into the stories of those lives, of her hearers. Some people would become angry, others merely distraught. Time wore on, as time always will, and still she continued spinning her stories, with more and more detail and wonder and anticipation and joy, to all those who would hear. The stories began to bring only joy, even when they would still occasionally, and always inadvertently, hit upon some small detail tucked away into the true life story, as into the past, of one or another of her hearers.

But to Akasha herself her storytelling, ever since that day of her early girlhood, only came on more and more naturally, so that while she was certainly never bored with her abilities, neither was she particularly challenged by them or herself changed. Above all, she began to value them for the kind of easy calm that the telling would always bring to her heart and to her mind. But it was much, much later, in fact as recent only as the telling of this selfsame story that Akasha began, for the first time in her life, to know (and to realize that she knew) things that other people just could not, or at least did not, know. She felt this at first in the depths of her strange orisons—'strange' because these orisons, these daily bursts or sparks of meditation, marked her out from the other members of her family and her friends surrounding her in her mid-sized town—and then later, and perhaps even more keenly, while relating her stories themselves, and last of all throughout all the parts of her daily life, including her nightly dreams. What kinds of things did Akasha know?

She knew the kinds of things that at first made her stories peculiar, and that had always been, on her part, unconscious and therefore unintentional. But then things began to be different: now she would make certain to, quite purposefully, addend a kind of prolegomena to her stories in which she knew the details would very readily rattle the cages (but this never too much) of any or all of her, shall we say, more wayward listeners. She had, of late, become a kind of moral instructress through the bewitching, enchanting details of her lovely yarns. But this she had never wanted, and it had never even crossed her mind as a purpose for her tales, yet when she began to see things, and to see people that she knew doing things, certain things of doubtful character or intent, it got on her nerves (and dwelt on her mind, in her thoughts) to such an extent that she found she could not resist the opportunity to raise some hairs on their neck.

Her stories themselves, though, continued to reflect their joyful sentiments and also began to ask questions that nobody present, neither her hearers nor she herself, had apparently ever once thought to ask: questions that increasingly approached unto subjects like the ones the old magician had talked to her about up on the mountain, just a little ways off the beaten path.

One morning, as Akasha was quietly sitting within her room, an image that she had never seen before floated into her mind, followed immediately by an overwhelming sensation of certainty that she now, and for the first time, understood what it was that the boy figurine that she had held onto for so long himself held out in the palm of his hand: it was a sculpture, too. A sculpture of something that she could not as yet understand, but a sculpture nonetheless, and of the very image, to her senseless, now pressing its way into her mind's eye: a lotus blossom, with a kind of strange bird rising up from its center. In her mind she then saw very vividly a blue fire, and then all else suddenly went blank.

After pausing to take in a deep breath, Metaxaeus held his hand out, palm open, to finally reveal the secret which he had so long been keeping to his father and mother. They gasped in unison. "Son" said his father immediately, "Where did you get that? Do you have any idea how many days in the fields that small piece of sapphire could save me from?" And when his mother spoke next, she said, too. "Son, how have you obtained these precious materials? Do you realize how much money that piece would fetch at a jeweler's shop, in the nearest city?" Yet Metaxaeus pretended not to notice what they had said, and was still reveling in their initial gasps, before finally asking, "Don't you two see what this is? I have done this with my own hands." Now they each leaned in to examine more closely the object that had caused their initial astonishment, just before the moment of their mutual consternation. And when they looked again they were even more impressed than they had been at first: the detail: the handiwork: all so lifelike and real. Lifelike enough, in fact, to cause in them both, suddenly, a bizarre kind of fluttering in the chest—after all, what was this creature coming to be, out of the very blossom held open, and held fast, in the very hand of their very own son? It was on fire. Quick, he will be burned! No, it was not on fire: impossible. It was only a bird, in miniature, carved out of a gem, and emerging from a piece of white stone, for all the world like that of a lotus blossom. It was, with first gasp and heart-flutters notwithstanding, the single most impressive thing either of them had ever seen. Ever.

The next day, after his time spent sitting beside the well, but still early in the morning, Metaxaeus left home with the blessing of his father and mother.

Traveling overland to the capital city of his region, Metaxaeus quickly found that the constant walking did wonders for his thoughts, and that the same contemplative moods which he had come to enjoy as the result of his daily practice by the well, could just as easily be enjoyed on foot traveling over the hills and on into some of the more mountainous passages through which his journey took him. Unable to read, he had brought with him no books, and therefore there were only the hours, the days and the nights both full, to maintain a kind of study of himself, always alertly peering into the ways of his soul.

Once he arrived in the city he knew that all he needed to do was to give things some time, and that then his soul, or the world, would somehow lead him to the place he needed to be. And once there, he would have to try on his own to find the work that he desired and which could support him until the day when his fame as a worker in stone had grown to the point that would make it possible for him to travel triumphantly back home, in comfort and in joy, to his family and his village.

As yet none of Metaxaeus' desires exceeded this one simple wish: to make a triumphant return home to his family, and to his village.

That night Metaxaeus camped high above the capital city, which was only a small speck of clustered and glowing lights along the valley floor, with the great river flowing straight through the midst of the city far below. It was now only a single day's march down from the high mountains that he had had to cross on his long journey to get here. But as he fell asleep, his dreams that night were unusually vivid, and troubling—in them he saw himself traveling on to a still farther country, traveling along by the current of the great river and into the next region with its own city and even beyond that, but this was not what really troubled him. For he also saw, in his dreams that night, perched high up in the mountain passes, as though asleep in an aerie, the same image that often came to him: that of his small phoenix-sculpture, only now it began to grow mightily in size to where it had become altogether fearsome to behold and came alive in new ways which he had not yet known or seen whilst all the while continuing to grow larger and yet larger until it seemed to Metaxaeus in his dreaming to become at last just what it was (that is, on some level, just what it had always been, at the center of its mystery)—a kind of emblem or image of the universe itself, and all a sort of fiery transparency made molten and alive right through. But even this vision is not what finally troubled Metaxaeus the most, for he had long known, ever since the day he had found the materials for his figurine, that there was some kind of magic embedded into the meaning of these two symbols, when put together, the ethereal bird with the lotus flower. What finally troubled Metaxaeus the most was that just as the living emblem of his small work in stone reached its omega point in size, seeming to have grown into something like a key to all space, and the fiery heart thereof, it vanished entirely and left nothing in its place but the image of a girl, with wondering eyes. And later on, in days to come, as he would sometimes struggle to recall to his mind the image of that girl that he had dreamt of that night high up in the mountains above the capital city of his region and the great river, he found he could not remember anything about her aside from those curious, moving, and in-drawing eyes: her wondering eyes that then and now had the power to draw him in, such power to draw him in that he would feel himself melted, melted into her and into her alone. Like some curious and fearful thing in no way different from what he might imagine to be the fiery heart of the whole world's soul, had it one. Does the vast world have within it a soul of its own? If so, he suddenly felt certain, for him it would be centered in her and her wondering eyes.

This was the peculiar vision that Metaxaeus had the night before his final descent into the city, and a glimpse of the questions that it wrought in him. Too it was the reason that he had, overnight, become troubled. For it was as if his own soul had been subtly translated into a new and embodied paradox, difficult to bear and opposite, yet beyond belief. Now, on the morning of his last departure down into the capital city of the great river, Metaxaeus realized with certainty that a new kind of trouble had for thereafter chosen to settle itself about his heart, having chiseled its way into his spirit, but for how long it must remain there, this troubling hope and uneasy gift, he did not as yet know.

BOOK III
A New Direction

Understandably, the idea for some new and farther pilgrimage had begun to forge itself into being in the soul of Metaxaeus, as a result of his unsettling dream of the girl with the melting eyes. He had grown restless in the course of a fortnight, and even his morning orisons (which he continued) and his laboring in stone, two usually unfailing sources of peace and calm, had ceased to bring him the quietude or relaxation that he had grown so accustomed to. That he used to depend on. All he could think of was the girl in his dreams. The fluid river of images that he was so used to observing still ran through his mind, but had now become concentrated around the image of those wondering eyes. There was little doubt about it, that he had been changed: his spirit felt to him as if it had been subtly yet distinctly transformed. And he knew that his thoughts were changing, too—suddenly he was beginning to reflect more and more on some lessons he had been given a long time ago, lessons about a mystery he had since hardly thought of and had only heard called spirit: spirit and its link to the Maker of the World. He found himself reflecting, too, on the significance of his thoughts at the time of the dream of the girl, and on the other images that had been there with him that night, about the curious meaning of the sculpture which he held always with him, its twin symbols, and about the visions of his traveling down the great river, and his questions having to do with a soul to the world, and whether there was one. What would such a thing be like? And what did all of these things, each occupying his mind at the same time, have to do one with another, if anything?

He then took to climbing high above the city in the evenings, where he could watch the sun make its way down in the sky and fall away behind the mountains on the other side of the long valley floor, as the lamplights would come gradually on in the city below. This scene above the city was the one ritual he had found which helped a little to becalm his anxious self, and his anxious thinking. Here he could rest from the work of the day, which he had been able to find easily and on his first day in the capital city, by displaying to the master stoneworkers a handful of carved trinkets, made from some stone found in the mountains, that he had had the opportunity and the time to sculpt whilst resting from his walking on the evenings of his journey. Anyways, it was here above the city, and while resting from his days' labors, in the evenings at sundown that he could at last let his mind and his soul settle down and peruse the new directions that were taking their shape in his heart. He could feel there the mysteries of new ways, ways new to him, churning and forming themselves, new and original thoughts about his life and its place in the wide world. But he did not yet know what to do: and perhaps he did not realize well enough how to ask the right questions so that he could better understand the truth about where to go next, and how, and when, and for what purpose. These were the questions inside to which he felt he needed the answers, before he could make the right decisions.

It was on one of these evenings, while sitting alone, and as usual far above the city, contemplating the sunset, its orange glow spreading the last light of day over the radiant distant ridgeline, withal the lines upon lines of spectacular, snow-capped mountains all floating away into the luminous distance, and the first stars of twilight rising empurpled into the night sky, that to Metaxaeus, perched quietly upon a shelf of rock high above the city, light years away from its day of laboring, there then came a gentle breeze, sudden enough to lift him from the midst of his reveries, his thoughts with their swirling questions, and to buoy him up into the vistas surrounding, the sun's lingering light, and to deliver to him—was it on the wind, or was it only in his mind?—the suggestion of a kiss....

That was when he reeled in the very midst of his burgeoning questions and for the first time felt that he understood their answer. He had been here for only two moons and already it felt as though these days of labor, and these evenings above the city, even when bathed in the sun's waning rays, were drawing on endlessly. Ordinarily, these times should have put him at peace, doing in the daytimes the work that he loved to do, and living in the far off city of his dreams, or at least, what seemed to have now suddenly become his olden dreams. What was it, then? What was the authentic cause of these new, silent, troubling, but nonetheless sacred-feeling thoughts, these newer dreams teeming away inside his increasingly restless mind? What was happening to him? What center within, or what center beyond, was all of this emanating from? In any event it was by dint of these questions, and their suddenly secret kiss, the gentle wind's mindful, merciful caress, that he thus knew that it was time for him to move again: and if necessary even to take with him his newfound mental busyness and the unending questions and find a guide to take him down the great river and on that journey to hope for a new calm while keeping his eyes open for helpful signs, whether arising in himself or appearing in the world. He would teach himself to trust this turmoil within for as long as it lasted, but as well he would trust in the great river's strange shows of synchronicity to let him know when he had found her, and to unfold the moment when the kiss received upon the wind, could then become true and so enter into his life.

He knew that he would have the river, and its mesmerizing current, day after day, to put his trust in and ultimately to answer his most pressing questions. But to think that hardly two months ago his only dream had been to travel to and live and work in the great capital city where he might find his fame and then, one day, return triumphantly to his home and to his family and their village. But now he felt that in the days which had passed new horizons had opened up in his soul and that to simply ignore those horizons might cause an inescapable kind of suffering to take hold of him for even the rest of his life; and he was youthfully wise enough to recognize that suffering without escape was the worst kind of suffering that there could be. As a matter of fact, Metaxaeus had begun to think that he might one day find a new home, either away or even far away from the village he had left behind, and in the backmost quarter of his mind he had even to ask himself whether or not he may ever again see his father and mother, and all this after a total of only three moons abroad and away from the place where he had grown up, the only place which he had ever known as home. What had happened to him? And where would he be able to find anew his solace?

BOOK IV
The Great River

Ever since the morning of her fiery vision concerning the sculpture held out in the hand of her boy figurine, Akasha had not been able to tell any stories, and had terrible trouble sleeping. Only she was right. She knew she was right. Somehow, she knew that the sculpture of the boy—or maybe it was a youth?— that she had hung onto for so long was a real person, somewhere. And now she knew, too, of the thing that he held out in the palm of his hand. It was itself a sculpture. In fact, it was a sculpture of the strange and fiery-blue bird radiantly emergent from the form of a white lotus blossom, that she had seen, vivid and precise, in her vision. What a curious image. Alas, since the morning of her vision her mind's eye had gone horribly blank. As was said, she could no longer tell to her townspeople or even to her own family any of her exciting stories, all suddenly vanished, but what was worse, their feeling vanished with them: Akasha enjoyed no calm. During the day, she felt only irritable and sleepy, and everything was even worse than that because, worst of all, she had absolutely no idea what had actually happened, to change everything so suddenly; and neither could she comprehend why. Her only solace was that, again, somehow she knew she was right: she knew for certain, within herself, that she was right about the tiny sculpture that she had kept for so long, and that she was right about this boy, this youth's reality, somewhere, and the reality of his own sculpture, however exceedingly strange: and she knew all of this with all the more conviction for the sudden disappearance of her calm, her abilities—this had to be significant. Still, even with all of her conviction, none of it answered the question of what she should do. In the short term, how could she regain her calm, even if not her storytelling prowess? And why, precisely, was it that she suddenly could not rely on a night's worth of rest, where had her peace actually gone to, and what was she supposed to do now? How was she to comport herself during all of this, and in the meantime? Eventually, in the hopes of it somehow helping her to be better able to tackle these questions, she took up the habit of going daily down to the banks of the great river, sitting beside its easy, sliding current and just wondering to herself about the many things she had on her mind. And she soon found that this new habit did in fact bring to her a measure of the kind of calm she was so used to enjoying within herself: the shores of the great river could momentarily restore the kind of peace that she had grown so used to being able to depend upon. So she made certain to go there daily, and as she continued this new habit, her periods of time spent along the banks of the river began gradually to increase until, soon, she found she would spend hours during the afternoons and on into the evenings, doing nothing but resting beside the banks of the river.

In her mid-sized town, Akasha, largely because of her early demonstrated talents of storytelling, was one of the few fortunate children who had been taught how to read, by the schoolmaster. So, now in these days spent whiling away the time peacefully by the river, she also grew into the habit of taking some books with her to read there along the shore.

One of the books she opened on one of these days spent along the riverbank, was the story of a man who was a healer. The book claimed it to be a true story: and, for Akasha, it was ever the stories that seemed to have the most amount of truth in them, even when not actually true in themselves (that is, true in their events), that she enjoyed and sought for the most. So now she began to take in this true story of the man who had once been a healer, and gently her mind began to unfold new questions to her, and ideas that she had never thought of before began to float their way into her imagination, like pieces of golden leaves, in the fall, gentled downstream on the huge current of the great river itself.

This man had, whilst he was still only a youth, wandered away from his home (with the blessing of his mother and father) to look for work in a distant city. He was an extremely gifted blacksmith, but after a very brief time in this work for which he demonstrated the most talent, he decided again that it was time for more traveling, only this time it was to be with the help of one of the ancient guides that have from time immemorial assisted travelers up and down and over and across the great rivers of the wide world. He decided to make his way down the slow arc of the great river itself—the very same river on whose banks Akasha now sat as she read the story. Eventually, he located a small village that could use the abilities of a gifted blacksmith, and whose people were amenable to having a stranger settle, and so for a season went on with his work. As it happened, however, a season soon evolved into a life. But what fascinated Akasha about this story was the detail, as if told from a firsthand account, of this man who became a healer's inner life, his inner life as he made his way down the great river and especially after he settled in his new home in the small village not far from the banks of the river. As it turns out in the tale, the healer had made a daily practice of sitting very still and very quiet for a time, a practice, of course, not unlike Akasha's own 'strange' orison, which she still did each and every morning. Beyond this, the healer referred to these sessions as his 'travels within,' and he there became accustomed to seeing strange sights, and experiencing feelings of deep peace. The part that drew Akasha in most of all, though, was a somewhat different sort of practice that he had apparently acquired while drifting daily down the current of the great river: he had learned to ask questions, formulated away down in his soul and then arising from a deep place there, of the great river itself and then to look out for signs as the answers to what he had asked that day would then appear most often along the banks of the river, as he and his guide would sift swiftly over the top of the moving waters on their way downstream. Naturally, Akasha began to wonder to herself whether the same thing could work, while sitting along the shores of the river: did the river itself have the answers to her questions, waiting to be provided if only she realized how to ask?

Later on and more towards the end of the book, there was a chapter that told brief accounts of other healers who claimed they had acquired the ability to travel throughout an invisible realm and there find, so as to either bring back or just to make whole again, broken and fractured or missing pieces of people's souls, thereby healing them from all varieties of sickness and disease. The final chapter, though, claimed that this particular healer featured in the book was different because neither did he know about, nor how to do, any of this business in another realm, but only realized, one day, that the more he sat quietly and went within himself and asked questions of the world through the depths of his soul, that the people which he then came into contact with would always insist that they felt better in his presence than anyplace else, until soon some of them even began to swear that they had been healed by the strange but peaceful blacksmith. Ultimately, then, it was the blacksmith-healer himself who was as mystified by the how or the wherefore of the claims of healing, as anyone. At this, Akasha again wondered to herself if she could one day learn to have a similar gift, and yet she understood that if she could that she would then do her very best to put that magic into her stories, so that the people who listened to her tell them would feel as though they had not felt so well in years.

But for now, she would have to teach herself to direct her questions into the heart of the great river, and what answers in return? For that, she felt she had all the time in the world.

Metaxaeus found his riverguide and commenced his journey. Traveling down the great river, without a clue, as yet, as to where precisely he was going or when he would be stopping in his quest. It was the turmoil inside and the fountain of questions there, that he was interested in finding the answers to, and for this particular endeavor he, too, felt as if he had all the time in the world.

BOOK V
Maya

For a split second, Metaxaeus could have sworn that his guide had winked at him, but even if so, it happened so quickly that he decided to forget about it. In any case, he had just pulled from his coat pocket the small sculpture of the phoenix in the lotus. He had made a kind of ritual out of keeping this thing, this bird-and-blossom object of his, out of his pocket and in his hands, as they made their way down the river. At first he had feared that, doing so, he might accidentally drop the object into the river, but then as he thought about it some more he wound up convincing himself that there was more risk that it might slip from his coat pocket, and besides, he wanted above all, these days, to contemplate the mystery of this little figurine, with its two startling symbols made one, wrought with his own hands; and he wanted to look back on the lesson he had received, once upon a time, on the day that he had initially been given these two precious stones....

Metaxaeus had been only a boy, when one day while he was in one of the small marketplaces of a neighboring town, accompanied by his family, of course, he lost track of his mother and father, and was suddenly confronted by an old lady whom, he immediately had within himself the feeling, must have been some kind of a strange old bird, either a healer or else a witch. But as soon as she smiled at him she seemed kindly, so when she offered to him her hand he did not refuse, but instead followed along behind her until they both came to the edge of the town, making their way from there a short distance into the forest until they came upon a kind of worn hut that may even have been her home. She told him that her name was Maya (which meant nothing to him), and she even had knowledge of his own name, so difficult for most people to pronounce, which she said aloud to him, saying the *x* as the sound of a *z*, as it is supposed to be said, "Metaxaeus."

More than anything else, this elderly lady, Maya, talked: she kept on for what must have been hours but curiously felt more like minutes than anything else. After they had passed over the threshold of her worn hut she gave Metaxaeus to eat a kind of crumbly green herb of the Earth, a variety he had never seen before, nor had ever seen since, which he did take and ate. He remembered feeling a bit lightheaded, but that was all. So she talked to him, for hours, while he sat there, still, and all the while on the edge of feeling dizzy, he received a kind of series of lessons from the old woman: lessons, what else to call them? She told him that as he grew older he may begin to suffer more in the midst of life, and that life was normally very hard, for everybody. But that there existed a way, a kind of path, away from and out of this suffering and that for those few fortunate enough to find it and to walk it every day of their lives that after a while, sooner or perhaps later, who could say for sure, the evils of the world would for them then become a thing less real, that the world itself surrounding them may then become only a kind of blessing to all those who walked along this way or this path, this pathway. Good things and rare, some foreseen, some unforeseen (she said), might then befall a person and unfold for them in their daily lives. She said that in order for Metaxaeus to find this pathway and remain on it, he must study himself and learn to know himself very well, and that truly the only way to do this was to learn to sit very quietly alone with oneself for long periods of time until one had learned the art of witnessing the quietening of one's thoughts, usually so intrusive as regards what would otherwise be one's calm, one's peace or tranquility. And she had an expression for this state, this ideal state of tranquility within oneself: she called it ataraxia, the freedom from disturbance. Still she taught of the mystery of this way: she hinted that ultimately one, again, only by discovering this path, might come to know of an invisible thing connected to our consciousness and itself conscious of everybody and everything in the world: she even said that this invisible thing was itself the Maker of the World, the Maker of the world in each of its facets both visible and invisible, and this she called spirit. At this Metaxaeus' dizziness increased until he suddenly fell into a swoon, falling dead asleep right there on the floor of the old woman's worn hut and hearing only some final murmurings about rebirth and transformation and the importance, for the boy, of a blue fire... "Carve," she whispered to him, "Learn with your whole soul how to carve in stone and eventually you will understand all that I have tried to say to you."

When Metaxaeus awoke, it was to the gentle shaking of his father's hands in a glade just beyond the marketplace of the town. His head felt very clear, and on the trip home he discovered in his pocket a pair of small stones, the one burning blue and clear as though lit by a kind of strange light from within, which he later learned to call sapphire, and the other a small white oval perhaps not much bigger than the pad of his thumb. This one he knew then was alabaster. In days to come, Metaxaeus gave little or no heed to the old woman's advice about learning how to quieten one's thinking, and he only thought of her sharp words to him as he was drifting off to (or already deep in the midst of?) sleep: to learn how to carve in stone, and to do so with his whole soul. What could even this mean, to learn to do something with his whole soul?

Perhaps Metaxaeus would never have thought much about the rest of Maya's words to him that day, were it not for a dream, and then a series of dreams, that he had one night not long after his family's visit to the small neighboring town with its monthly marketplace. In his original dream, Metaxaeus saw himself being pursued by a large overgrown snake, nay a veritably giant serpent, and, frightened out of his wits, he ran and ran and ran until at long last he could not possibly run another step. At this juncture, though, a curious thing happened: Metaxaeus stopped in his tracks and turned to face the serpent, only as he did so, his body began to rise up into the air and to float there, hanging in space, and then the dream-self did something that he, his waking self, would never have thought to do: he there, hovering in mid-air, folded his legs into a cross-legged position and began to take up a sort of floating posture of meditation, at which moment in the dream the serpent began to dissolve into the aether, into the dream nothingness from which it had originally sprung: it did not exist.

It was this dream that prompted Metaxaeus to reflect on the old lady's words about the relative disappearance of evil in the lives of all those who are fortunate enough to have found the Path. And it was from that morning on that he had taken up his practice of sitting daily down beside the old well on the outskirts of his village.

Then, though, a new series of dreaming emerged, and at first and for a long time afterwards he would always have the same sensation of lightheadedness that he had had in the worn old hut of the forest that day. Of these dreams, this new series of dreams, we have already heard much—into his mind would come, in varying degrees of verisimilitude or lifelikeness, the twin images of the lotus flower and the emergent fiery bird, which, like the name of the sapphire stone itself, he soon learned to call a phoenix, the strange and rare and mystical bird that would periodically burst into flames only to then recreate itself from its own ashes.

All of this, along with the girl, Metaxaeus tried to think about now as he was carried farther and farther away from the capital city of his region, from his home in the village, and from the land of his boyhood, buoyed along by the current of the great river all the livelong day betwixt and between the rising and setting of the wonderful sun, and the turning of the Earth. Home was now none other than this silvery ribbon, anon sliding through what only seemed like a vast green isle, emerald. When the first stars would begin to appear, overhead in that overspreading vault of the twilight sky, and begin to come up above the treetops along the riverbank, Metaxaeus' riverguide would pole them easily to the shore and they would make their camp, looking up all night long into the face of a thousand distant suns.

BOOK VI
The Passionate Earth

Akasha sat there along the banks of the great river, each afternoon on into the evening. She felt certain that she had figured out that if the cause of her peculiar unrest had its genesis in the same instant as her vision of the youth's sculpture, then that is exactly where she might do best to start from in her reasonings, her answering to herself of her own questions, all spiraling away for now in her soul. So she re-envisioned these things to herself, recalling them to her mind as best she could, as vividly. A sapphirine phoenix emergent from a white lotus flower: what could it mean? What did such a combination of symbols suggest to her mind, to her intuition, to her spirit? Could she relate it to any of the things she told about in her stories, or to anything, anything specific, that she had learned about in the course of her life, perhaps either in her daily morning prayers, her orisons, or even in the words of the old magician? Did the phoenix and the lotus blossom together have some bizarre, maybe ethereal or magical or at least symbolic connection to what little she knew of the spirit and the Maker of the World? Would it be possible to direct any of these questions—all of them?—into the heart of the great river? Akasha knew that the river was very old and therefore very wise, but how could it possibly have the power—where and when would it have learned such power?— to unfold for her the answers to such questions? How could it color in so many of the details, or make all of the correct connections? She did not know: but she was nonetheless resolved to try.

And immediately the great river seemed to deliver an answer: Akasha watched breathlessly as an enormous eagle plunged furiously down from the sky and into the precise center of a warbled reflection of the setting sun, drawing up from the great river a red and silver salmon, the fish now flashing golden in the air of the sun's waning light, whilst the eagle was already arcing away into the blue distance overhead with the still sparkling fish dangling between its talons—even more exciting than the thrall for her of this event, however, was the thought she found she suddenly simultaneously had as the bird crashed through the center of the river reflected sun: the mercurial ash of waters, scene of fire, scene of light: she seemed to realize, in that split second of time, agape, what would have to happen, how all things would have to be, in order for the universe to be whole, as it doubtlessly was. It was a feeling, only: but the feeling was like a total intuition, of which there could be no doubt: everything would have to be linked to everything else, making all things into one, in which an eagle or a phoenix could crash into water, rise up from ashes there, and at the same moment a fish could rise, a world could momentarily mount into flame, a sun could set, a girl could wonder, a river would flow, and a youth that she had never before seen could somehow have already been born years ago and yet once upon a time—space and time, might as well be worlds, away from her and even, most curious of all?, from himself—yet have been carved into a small piece of stone by the hand of a magus, or by the hand of God (for what difference could it make?) and she, she suddenly knew, might even be able to send to him somewhere a kiss from out of the depths of her own soul that would somehow have the uncanny power to sail out of time itself even, and find the boy, the youth, wherever, nay whenever he may be... and so she did so: Akasha at that moment, without hesitating, from the depths of her realization brought on by the action of the great river, blew to the nameless youth a kiss, and knew for certain that, someway, somehow it had already found him, somewhere outside of time. And then she resolved again to wait on the great river; she still had many more questions that she wanted to ask.

Akasha figured that from now on she would concentre her questions as much as possible, condensing them into one succinct query at a time, and then let the river respond, so that the inquiry would be narrow, no matter how broad the realization brought on by the river's response. So it was in this way that at the game of waiting she became even more skilled than she had generally been: sitting there, frozen, awaiting a sign from the great river, only after having asked it her question. Today the question at the forefront of her mind, the one that she most wished to have answered was: how could she be able to trust, as much as she would love to be able to do, in the majesty of life, without first understanding the meaning of her death? "This I would like to see be revealed to me, before asking any of the other things I would ask" she said to the river, murmuring softly to herself. At first, the response of the great river, to this question, seemed to be one of opacity, but then, and Akasha could hardly have said how she even knew it to be significant, the winds changed, causing at that moment a silent sweep of autumn leaves to release themselves from their boughs, tumbling through the air and into the river below in an oddly symphonic arc of being they tumbled, almost laughingly, into the waters below, which then of course swiftly carried them out of sight. At this, though she could not have explained why, Akasha at first felt haunted, but then quickly felt as though, for some reason, she might begin to weep, only had she wept they would not have been tears of sorrow, but rather tears of something infinitely beyond sorrow, something impossible to name, almost a kind of relief, but even then something far sweeter, far deeper even than relief. So this was the great river's answer to the riddle of death, and the feeling she now had inside herself was altogether impossible to describe: a curious mixture of shame and remorse that she could not understand the reason for, coupled with what must have been a kind of divine relief, beneath the shame or remorse, and finally the seemingly flat out impossible gnosis of an eternity, an intuition so strong and firm suddenly alive within her as though embedded straight into her heart, and all of this from a mere gust of winds, and the sweeping away of some leaves, along down that long current. "Alas, Great River, what don't we see?" She murmured wonderingly. Until at last she did weep, only now she wept out of joy and belief: that was twice now, and the great river had managed to respond to her each time: she knew that her soul was learning again, and that only with patience, would go on doing so.

She had not doubted that the river was old and very wise, but in days to come it showed to her again and again, in ways she never could have imagined, how it was always new, too, forever young and always ready to say some new thing to her about the most important questions she could conceive: it even taught her of the signal mystery of creation, that of rebirth, in that the great river with its ceaseless, sleepless flow was ever new, and therefore was itself being born again continually and that without any let at all. Besides, had not it already shown to her the phoenix itself, in that flashing fiery form of the great eagle dashing into the image of the sun upon the face of the waters? She garnered that all of creation must be like this: or at least the part that was in any way spiritual, that is, connected to the one Great Spirit: and, finally, what was there of creation, the whole, that was not connected to the one Great Spirit? Only our realization of this mystery depended upon our own being born again anew each day of our lives, and this, Akasha realized, was precisely what she had already been doing for so many years, every morning with her orisons, her meditation: this is what the magician had meant when he advised her to become still and to learn to go all the way within herself: this was the human being's mysterious way of becoming ash, of (one might even say) dying again and again, or bursting into a kind of invisible fire, only to rise again, anon, from one's own ashes, sacred and creative. This is what the symbol of the phoenix had meant, bursting into color: and that ground of the lotus flower, its meaning? That was the ground of our own being, of both creation and creative manifestation themselves, always present, always arising, always enabling to be born, so one could go on like that, dying daily, again and again only to be renewed from within, and discover that one was already one with the world, one with the whole world and could not ever be other than it. These were the mysteries that she, the girl Akasha, had long been on the fringes of, had long dallied along the edges of in the telling of her stories and in her repeated morning meditations, but now the longing of her heart was to at last enter there, and to enter there more fully, into the very blazing and etheric core of these invisible things, to have these silent sacred arch-mysteries all at once enter into the atmosphere of her soul, her calling and answering spirit, and finally to make their way thoroughly into the world vis-à-vis her Self, a kind of pure creative manifestation. This she wanted to know: to experience. She wondered. She felt suddenly certain: and she willed it: she would, if possible, learn herself into an altogether different being: she would realize how to transform herself into something divinely above being human, even, though ever more deeply human, too, and if she succeeded, she would then somehow prepare a way, before ever sleeping, to give her gift to the world, beginning with those nearest and dearest to her own heart, beginning, perhaps, with the as yet nameless youth.

At that moment, Akasha paused to hear, and to read as if on the wind—though was it only in her mind?—the word, spoken softly, yet to her ears as clear as a bell, 'Metaxaeus.'

Now, she believed, she even knew his name.

The great river never sleeps: its waters turn and flow, turn and flow again. It is ageless, timeless. An image of eternity: and ever an instance of now. Akasha, learning from this turning flow, taking from it her cue, and musing on its concert with her own soul, herself turned the image of the phoenix and the lotus over again and again inside the chamber of her mind, her psyche, her spirit, her soul. She did this for many days until at last she concluded that it must be an emblem of enlightenment, both its predictor and token, and a kind of ultimate entrance into the mystery, finally unfathomable, inscrutable, of creation itself. This was the Light of the Spirit and the Maker of the World, One, the subtle essence of the Earth, and the core of the cosmos, that shone into the soul of women and men: indeed, the passionate Earth a kind of wonderful jewel, and wonderful beyond naming, beyond all telling or saying, but the world, what was the world? The world, maybe, was a type of bezel, fit only for the becoming of men and women into that which alone is real.

Yes, and what is real? Only the light that finally dawns within. The music of the passionate Earth. Enlightenment. That was the meaning of her vision: and that, she assumed, could be the only meaning of the object: the sapphirine phoenix rising up from out of the generative matrix and ground of the white lotus flower. How long would she have to wait for that light: and how much did she still have to suffer? What was she? And who? And who was the magus whom she had met so long ago and who had given her such a gift, gift of storytelling, gift of insight, gift of wonder, gift of intuition, after all, the gift of herself; and where, as well, would this youth whom she knew to be real have himself discovered such a strange conjunction of symbols wrought into stone?

There is, always, more light to be shone.

In more of the days to come, the young woman began to think of her being as a kind of fountain, through which the Maker of the World Itself, the one ever invisible spirit, was continually pouring Itself forth. She now felt, because of her interaction with the great river, and also because of the answers now arising to reside within her, an influx and a rush of peace, and joy, and gratitude, and energy, and a sense of complete well-being; she now felt as if she had been transformed into a whole and harmonious self, conscious, willing, miraculous, awake, and undivided from the world, at peace and centered in the universe.

She even wondered, had she become indestructible? For this was the feeling she had. Had she changed so much, already? Could she really expect nothing else from her path but the world's blessings? She felt no fear of evil, and no anxiety over troubles. And her heart was on fire; her whole heart was as nothing if not on fire.

She felt as though, that in all the wide world, there could not exist a being anywhere whose eyes she was not ready to meet, and meet again.

BOOK VII
Dream of the Wind

Metaxaeus figured that he might as well give it a try: what could it hurt? He would send his name out on the wind, and if it be that she were listening, somewhere, maybe she would hear it. After all, had not he already received a kiss? Perhaps he was crazy, and such games played with himself would never get him anywhere, but still he resolved to try. "Metaxaeus," he whispered, feeling foolish: what was he doing? Only then he imagined that something in the wind had, at the mention of his name, picked up just a bit, so he said to himself again, a bit louder this time, "Metaxaeus." And this time there was to be no doubt: along the river came a sweeping gust of wind, scattering many of the golden leaves of autumn from their boughs hanging out over the great river, so that they settled onto the wide current and there went rushing on from sight. "Metaxaeus." Shouted Metaxaeus, and the wind blew stronger still: he may as well have been the Maker of the World, or the Great Spirit itself, operating a bellows: still he shouted his name over and over again as loudly as he could muster and always into the winds, until at last he only whispered, "Metaxaeus." Once more and desisted. It was then that he felt the winds blow through his heart: the air above and surrounding the river became very still, but in his chest Metaxaeus felt a wind rushing with great force, like a gale. How could it be? What was this? What was he experiencing? For a minute it occurred to him that he could be dying, but then it stopped....

He woke with a start, his riverguide jabbing him in the chest with a stick in order to interrupt his wildly tossing in his sleep. The sun was already up. He had been dreaming: in his dream he had stood there on the banks of the river and summoned the winds with the mere utterance of his name as though he himself were the Maker of the World, the one Great Spirit, and only because he had wanted her to know his name.

Freed from his slumber, Metaxaeus arose and swiftly readied himself for another day of traveling down the great river. Mostly, he had found that as the days passed he only felt dreary and, as it were, adrift. Now his nightly dreams were beginning to become even stranger than usual. Why had he fancied his name would be sent out on the winds? Come to think of it, why had he fancied, to begin with, that somehow he had received a kiss of that kind, and that it had been meant for him? He was growing more and more doubtful.

"You should not brood so much," said his guide to him at that moment: and it was the first words he had spoken in a fortnight spent gliding down the river.

"I am not brooding: I am thinking."

"Yes, I see. Too much thinking is maybe not so good. Maybe you think too much, ever think of that?"

"You are talkative all of a sudden."

His guide laughed. "I am just concerned, that is all. And usually it is not my business to be concerned, but take last night—that was some dream you were having. I have never heard the winds howl so much as that."

"What are you talking about? What winds?"

"You act like you do not know. Last night, while you were turning about in your dreams, the winds in this place came as mightily down the river's channel as I have ever seen. I was afraid we would have the trees toppled upon us. You slept through all of this."

Metaxaeus looked away. He did not know what to say: it seemed extraordinary to him that the winds should have blown so wildly in the night, what with the dream that he had had.

The ensuing days passed by without any more remarks from his guide, and Metaxaeus was content to carry on with his "brooding," his watching of the flowing land, and his ongoing observations of his own thoughts. Truth be told, his spirits had risen a little following the mystery of the winds: could there have been something more than meets the eye to his dream that night, aside from the obvious cause of the winds outside? He felt like there was a connection: perhaps he had delivered his message, after all, he found himself thinking, though that thought seemed to be the craziest of all. No, of course he had only been dreaming.

As for synchronicity or coincidence, and all other sign-posts made evident to travelers in the vast environment of the great river, Metaxaeus no longer knew what he had been expecting to see: the great river day after day seemed to want to show along its banks only trees and more trees—the surrounding forest fully engulfed the lands through which they were traveling. But the woods were beautiful: the crisp autumn was dazzling in its array of colors, like a variety of bright flames. While at night the stars shone above in myriad points of light.

BOOK VIII
The Rains

The first spits of rain began to arrive on the wind. The old woman looked unabashed towards the oncoming storm, unfrightened and unworried. She unhurriedly undid the one button from a small leathern satchel before removing from it a thing she had long kept put away high above a cluttered space of shelves housing old wares, as it were hid beneath an upturned bowl. This object from the leathern satchel she now bent down to place between her feet and set into the mud on the riverbank just beside the waters of the great river: she knew that momently the rains would come, and that with them the waters would rise until this object would be for a time muddily lost from view, but she also knew who would find it when, some days later, it emerged again. And that is what caused her to smile to herself, before turning away, and that not a moment earlier than the first sheets of true rain began with the force of their drops to dapple the mud beside the onrushing river.

BOOK IX
Legendary Stone

Akasha blinked her eyes awake in the streaming rays of the morning sun's first light. Light like new wine poured from the olden cruse of the world: aetheric vessel. She rolled drowsily from bed, and then looked out from her window disbelievingly, for the days of rain had finally gone, leaving the skies washed and blue and the surrounding fall all once again in the atmosphere of flame, still damp and yet blisteringly new with its everywhere burnished leaves. Leaves everywhere piling into drifts along the ground of the forest, leaves still on the trees, leaves yet dripping with the recent rains, and scores of leaves of course always rushing away down the current of the great river. On this morning even the scent of the old forest could be vividly discerned wafting its way into the atmosphere of her home.

After the days of rain had left, it took a few more days for the waters of the great river to return to their normal depth and to become once more unmuddied. The last day of rain had been on the first day of the week, and it was on the sixth day of the same week that Akasha's eyes fell on a thing seeming to glint at her from just beneath the surface of the river, whatever thing that it was was as yet still half buried in the mud on the riverbottom, not far from the shore.... For some strange reason, a blaze of curiosity seized her, and without even bothering to roll up the legs on the pair of canvases that she was wearing she plunged straight into the shallow water of the river's edge, gasping for a moment at the feeling of the cold on her legs, and then began savagely to unearth the small object she was certain she had glimpsed glinting out at her from just beneath the river's muddy floor. And there it was: she had it in her hands! What was it? It was...the first thing of its kind that she had ever seen; it was a marvel. Her eyes widened greatly at the possibility of what she now held in her hands: how? How was this even possible at all? You see, when she had yet been very young, one of the more childish stories she had told for a season was that of a little girl (a little girl whom at that time she had of course imagined to be none other than herself) who could find her way through any labyrinth by virtue of a little token that she held always with her: a little token not much larger than the size of a coin, and shaped into the shape of a glass phial that held, locked away into an impenetrable core, a lightseed: a seed of light that would glow mightily in the dark depths of the themselves impenetrable mazes that the girl would anon find herself cast away into the centers of, only impenetrable but for this tiny core of light, locked securely away into the center of its magical phial, that would glow softly whenever she made the right choice, moving along in the appropriate direction within the caves or dungeons. So, phial of magic: phial of light: she held this thing in her hands, and it did glow there, in the cusped palms of her open hands. She simply stared, wonderingly, at this object, until she at last began to ask herself what other magical properties it might possess; and this thought seemed to cause the thing to glow even more lucidly. At that moment she had within herself an insurmountable thought, 'What if it were to shatter?' Could it break? And if it did break, how strong of a light would that little lightseed within then prove itself to be? She would never come to know the answer to that question; for she knew then on the inside, like a rock, like a diamond or any otherwise adamantine substance, that this phial could never break: this magical locket of light could not ever be broken, could not ever be suffered to fracture or split: it was itself perhaps none other than that adamant of myth, legendary stone, seed of light, imprisoned in glass, splendorous....

The thing Akasha had found was not a dream: it continued to glow there, wherever it were either set or kept, as softly, as constantly, as real as anything else. She marveled and marveled again. She felt as if although she had already encountered and experienced strange things in her young life, that this was different from them all. She took to keeping it with her person at all times, and as she did so she felt like it were a kind of indestructible vigil that she carried with her. Her heart fluttered when she thought of it: what if the lightseed that she now kept in her pocket was combined with Metaxaeus' statuette, what if that seed of light inside the small phial of her keeping were somehow forged into the center of that sapphire gemstone, the phoenix? What then? Would such a thing then become a symbol of the fin de la fin of evolution itself? She could not imagine. What could it create? What was this that she was dreaming? Where had this thing come from?

BOOK X
On Towards the Sea?

"You need to make a decision," his guide said to him from across the fire one night. "Either you must look for your kind of work in the next town: or we will be traveling all of the way to the city by the sea. Not even the great river goes on forever."

The sea! Metaxaeus had never even thought that they were so close to the sea. In his mind he equated the city by the sea with the great wonders of the world. Were they really so close? But then he thought, alas, what then of the girl that he believed himself to be seeking?

"We need to go back. We need to travel back to the town which we passed during the days of rain. There is somebody there that I must find: and I am suddenly certain that that is where she must be."

"You want to go back? What are you talking about?"

"I am looking for somebody, and I am telling you, that nothing I am doing makes any sense if I do not find her. We have to turn around and go back upriver until we come again to the one town we passed over during the rains, when we decided that it would be better to use the rushing waters to speed us on our way."

At this his riverguide only sighed deeply, as though he had heard precisely this kind of story before, but then he said, "Okay, we go back. We turn around tomorrow."

"Once I have found who it is I am seeking, she and I can travel to the city by the sea, together." And in his mind Metaxaeus thought to himself, "Maybe we can even find a home to live in, somewhere along the coast of the great ocean...."

"Besides," Metaxaeus again mentioned to his guide, "Soon the snows will be here, and I hear that the towns on the river are warmer for travelers than the inns by the sea, where the winds can be fearsome every day."

"That is true," his guide agreed.

BOOK XI
Light and the Body

The weather over the following days was as favorable for late autumn as could be hoped for in any story in which lovers are to meet.

Metaxaeus and his guide had no trouble navigating their way back up the waters of the great river, and their at last approach to Akasha's town only took them a few more days, days, however, of arduous rowing to make their way against the current of the great river.

All of this whilst Akasha herself for the most part remained in thrall to her magical phial: she felt that she had even begun to discover some of its secrets. And, given what these were, the appropriateness that she had dredged it up from the bottom of the great river itself, which had been so generous with its answers to her questions, and with its teachings, was not lost on her. She had learned that she could ask it questions, and that then, based on whatever thought or series of thoughts that she observed herself to be having at the time of the particular question, it would then either glow more brightly or fade almost even to darkness in response to her thoughts, as though in sync or in rhythm with the very stream of her consciousness. This phenomenon was what had led up to her certainty that, whatever else it was, it was intelligent, too: it could answer questions. In that, it was like a living thing. This phial of light, entrapped piece of adamant, lightseed, and light within light, could answer for her any question that she would have. And it was this power that was too much for her to bear: this itself became the reason that she refused to ask it anything, with one exception: she would, each morning, and directly following her orison, ask it whether she could expect to meet the young man of her dreams, Metaxaeus, on that day or not that day.

Until today, she had each day received a dormant response from what had become to her like her very own talisman, this small object of concentrated light with its constant keeping vigil. The response she received on this morning, however, was something that she was entirely unprepared for....

Sitting there, on one cushion, with her legs folded beneath her, and her magical talisman resting beside her on the old wooden floorboards of her bedroom, Akasha asked it her question, and then watched in wonder and a rising anticipation as the light proceeded to issue, at first very gently, almost lovingly, and as though tenderly, but issued without ceasing, until she could no longer see anywhere within that light the contours of the phial itself, only an expanding orb of light with a kind of extraordinary density: but for the temperature, of which there was none, or if any only the gentlest warmth, she would swear she were peering into the heart of a star, into the bright heart of a star being born anew right there upon the floor of her room. But the light continued to grow, continued to ease itself into the atmosphere until it began with its sphere to engulf Akasha herself, at which event she felt more pleasantly alive, and more blissfully at peace in the present than she could recall having felt at any time before, until even her body, at first just her extremities and limbs and then ultimately the very center of her torso, her stomach and heart, all began to feel radiantly awake, blissfully alive. She felt she was having a spiritual experience, engulfed by light, until at last everything flashed into a blinding white, brighter even than the sun, and when the light then just as suddenly dispersed, she found she was elsewhere, not in her room, but high above the Earth, peering down at the silvery contours of the great river itself, able to see even the already snowy mountains in the distance, floating above everything, above all, bodiless, radiant, looking down now at the great river upon which made its way, struggling against the current, a small raft with two passengers, a riverguide and the youth of her heart, Metaxaeus. She knew him immediately. She was able to study him for what seemed like an eternity: she was able to move all around him and to pervade the space in every direction and always with her, ever-present, the light, light everywhere, why couldn't he see? She saw the handsome face of a youth, a face without lines, and the muscular back and arms arched over the arduous business of rowing upstream, against current, and she saw the aged face of the riverguide, a face heavy with lines, though even this face, from her present perspective in the surrounding space, seemed itself heavy only with lines of grace: and then, even in this her deep peace, her own tour through space, she started, because the riverguide, she would only have sworn, winked at her, as though he had espied somewhere in the center of airy space itself her own eyes, suddenly, and only for an instant, looking straight into them: and then the whole experience was over, she was back in her room, on her cushion, and the light from her phial was softly waning away.

Metaxaeus stood and stamped his feet on the rocky shore of the river, taking turns massaging with his hands the aching places behind each of his upper arms, and feeling the tight knot that had formed in the center of his back, both painful from having rowed upriver for several days. The sun still stood high in the sky, near to its zenith, and his guide told him that the girl's town was only a short footpath's distance away. But he wanted now, for a minute or for a while, and before wandering away towards the town and towards, he hoped, the girl in his dreams, to take a short time to reflect on his days spent combing his way down and up the stream of the great river. He did not feel as though he had experienced the kind of spiritual lessons, synchronistic, coincidental, or otherwise, which he had anticipated when setting out down the river, but now as he stood here on rocky soil and gazed up at the sun in its midheaven, and felt the ache of his muscles, the effects from the work of his body, it was then that he noticed that his mind, his self felt as it were unclouded by doubts or by misgivings of any kind: he felt only the thrill of anticipation at his perhaps encountering the girl that he had thought so much about and had, truth be told, thought almost solely about ever since the night of his vision of her in dreams, not to mention the evening of the kiss sent out on the winds. He felt his own readiness and anticipation in a physical way: he felt its presence in every cell.

Words are not adequate to do justice to the sense of elation that Akasha felt at the conclusion of this experience. What had just happened? She knew what she had seen, and what it must mean, but she could not understand how. Was it the power in her amulet that did this; or was it, perhaps stranger still, some power of her own? In any event, this had been more than a vision: she had, for a few moments, and moments then that had felt like an eternity, dwelt above the Earth, nay in and around and over and through the Earth; she may as well have been the Earth, the skies of the Earth, the space both surrounding and pervading, all one. And now all she had to do was wait. Now she would wait for Metaxaeus and when he was here she would tell him about everything: about the magus and his words to her and her orisons and storytelling and dreams and visions and the great river and sending to him her kiss and even receiving his name as though in return on the winds and about the amulet, the phial of adamant, core of light and lastly about her experience this morning. And what would he, himself, have to tell her in exchange? What gifts or stories had he that she could not yet imagine? She felt as though the hero of one of her own stories, stories she had told most naively when only a small child, was about to walk out from one of those stories and simply take her by her waiting hand. She could not wait; she must; she resolved she would not budge; but she changed her mind! And with that she flew to the shores of the river!

Metaxaeus had spent more than enough time on a rock, thinking, and thinking again, and then when once having finally come to the end of all his thoughts, thinking some more, for yet a little while. Now enough was enough. He knew he had nothing to bring to her; no gift that he could give. He stood up nonetheless and went finally back to the river once more, where he both thanked and dismissed his guide, paying for the trip and each man patting the other amicably upon the opposite shoulder as they both smiled and shook hands. He then turned to find the footpath that would take him to the town and, he hoped, to his new life.

They met, as it happened, walking along on the same path, she one way, and he another; she to the shore of the great river, and he on into her town....

BOOK XII
Meeting

They both stopped in their tracks, and smiled. They approached each other like that, facing one another on the trail, with neither one of them wishing to be the first to look away from the other's eyes, until when they each stood near enough, she said, simply, "Metaxaeus."

And then a long while seemed to elapse in which he did not find any words to say, until she finally spoke, again, and said, "Let us talk, and you can rest. You are tired, and my family has in our home a room. Besides, you will be wanting to know my name: I am called Akasha." Now Metaxaeus' face flushed to a deep shade of red, because he realized then that he had not even thought to ask of her her name, but then he regained just enough poise to whisper tenderly into her ear, "Akasha."

Their eyes shone very brightly.

One of the first things that Metaxaeus realized about Akasha, as soon as he was able to get by her, as it were, melting wondering eyes, was the sheer force of her beauty: he found that he could not take his eyes off of her, and that her beauty had in it a note of regality that seemed far beyond her years. She, for him to behold, was literally breathtaking. To look at her and to touch her, just to be near her, made him feel inside himself precisely the same sort of elation, that he could only recall having felt, though at no time specific, in his early childhood, when he was still just a youngster, maybe as when, for instance, he was in the presence of a new and wondrous place. And yet, he also felt nearer than ever to being a man, to being wholly a man and no longer a child, indeed no longer even a youth. To have her all to himself seemed to him like a kind of impossible wonder, like a dream or a miracle.

And Akasha, for her part, felt just the same way. When she was with Metaxaeus, she could think of nothing else aside from how good it felt to be surrounded by his arms, or to feel on her skin the gentle brush of his cheek: this alone was like nothing she had ever experienced before. Just to look on him was enough for her to know on the inside of herself, away down in her heart, that she was no longer just a girl, though she might still feel the same sense of elation.

"I heard your name on the wind, and then I even saw you coming," she said to him one night as they lay together in her room. "Impossible." He said, "I only dreamt that I had sent my name out to you on the winds, but if you heard it and you knew it, then I guess that it must be true."

In the ensuing days, and hours, after they had met each other walking in different directions on the little footpath down to the river, up to the town, the two of them spent all of their waking time discussing everything there was to think of or to recall about their lives, and about their peculiar separate roads leading up to one another, their meeting. There was still so much that neither one of them could completely understand, or even entirely be expected to. Metaxaeus, for his part, was joyed that Akasha had had so much more success learning from the great river than had he, on his journey. And when Akasha told him of how she had perceived that the riverguide had winked at her, while she was having her out-of-body experience, Metaxaeus had much the same instinct as he had had on that day when he himself had thought for a moment that his guide had winked over at him and his sculpture, that is, to forget all about it on account that she must surely have imagined such a slight thing. However, when she insisted, and said that it had not really been so slight a thing at all, they could only wonder.

Of course, she revealed to him the small sculpture that she had kept for so many years, at which he could only stare in a state of near bewilderment, as well the phial of light, adamantine still, and glowing softly at the touch or even the presence of Metaxaeus; and he showed to her the thing that he had made: at last she was able to see with her own eyes the phoenix in the lotus, and it was even more impressive in person, altogether dazzling in its verisimilitude, almost even than the vision she had had of it.

What more was there to say? It was a source of astonishment, of true amazement, to each one of them that they had found each other thus, with so much mystery woven into the very fabric of their coming together. Mostly they just wondered: what could it mean? Although they were so happy, just being together, that they could not think, for a season, at least, what all kinds of questions they perhaps ought to be asking themselves. Being so young, was not love always like this, for everybody? Yes and no. You see, first there is the need to be able to look at what ultimately they themselves would have to come to realize, to be and to know. And the way things happened it turned out to be another dream—what else?—that changed everything.

BOOK XIII
Another Journey

In the dream, Metaxaeus and Akasha were making their way, slowly, up into the high country, arduously up and away into the mountains covered with snow to the cave dwelling of an old hermit, a man rumored to be the sage of the region, an old man tutored in the ways of the spirit. They themselves neither one knew what it was that they were seeking, nor understood yet what it was that they ought to be looking for. They were weary and hungry and cold: their bodies had long since been telling them both to go back down the mountain, to turn around and live in the city by the sea. When they finally arrived at the door of the dwelling, a place seemingly carved out of the rock, it was near dark, inside a fire burned, and hovering there in the light of the flames was a face that in Akasha's mind, in this Akasha's dream, blurred together with the face of the magus she had talked to when a girl, and with the face of Metaxaeus' riverguide who had perceived her in the midst of her out-of-body experience on the day that Metaxaeus himself had finally arrived on the little footpath leading up to her town. Lastly, however, and strangest of all, the face of this sage cavedwelling high in the mountains seemed to transform into Metaxaeus' own face, the face she had already come to know so well, only now in this her dream it were as though wizened by years and years of aging, or weathered by days on days of wind and rain and sunlight and snows. And then she woke up.

The first thing she noticed, after coming awake from her strange dream, was the snow falling softly beyond the walls of her room, outside her window, a land freshly covered in white, yes on this very morning the year's first snows.

Akasha lay there awaiting Metaxaeus (who went to sleep in another room of this the house of her family) and watching the snowfall, thinking of her dream, trying to listen to what her heart told her about its meaning. Where would they be off to, now? To where would they have to make their way when all that her heart longed to do was to stay this way, and to stay here, forever and forever? What would Metaxaeus think about her dream, when he longed so much to visit and live in the city by the sea? Was this dream real enough that they should go wandering away towards the hills, and on up into the high country? Her heart told her that it was. She reached for the small phial which she had made into an amulet, tying on to it a small leather string that she could then keep tied around her neck. She asked it her question, whether or not she should trust in the dream's vision of a journey high up into the distant mountains: and surely enough, this small lightseed locked away within a glassworked bottle glowed gently, unmistakably there in her hands. Now only to talk with Metaxaeus, and begin making preparations.

BOOK XIV
Quest

After having exchanged their good-byes with Akasha's parents, Akasha and Metaxaeus shouldered their packs and set their feet on the old road heading out of the town and faced themselves towards those mountains in the distance. The old road would take them through two small villages along their way into the high country in which they could be sure to find lodging: an overnight stay and some drink to warm the stomach after moving through the season's suddenly aching cold. The entire trek should take no more than a fortnight, and once up into the mountains they would have very little idea where to look for either shelter or for whoever it was that they were seeking: hopefully, this sage would be expecting them, and would somehow find them himself, before it got to be too late.

Walking along the old road, and both huddled in their sheepskin cloaks against the bitter cold, Metaxaeus and Akasha wondered aloud about where they were headed, and what they could likely expect from an old hermit sequestered away up in the mountains, even despite the prospect of a frighteningly harsh winter. They could each remember being tutored once, she by the magus alongside the mountain path and he by the old lady named Maya inside the confines of a worn old hut, but each of these instances had taken place a long time ago when Metaxaeus and Akasha were still children, and both had been very brief. What were they in for up in the mountain passes? What sorts of things were they bound to learn? The prospect of discovery was one that, in any event, they both agreed was very thrilling; and in this they were like-minded, that they could appreciate the opportunity to be instructed in the deep ways of truth, in the ways of the spirit of which they had both pondered, and that seemed to have done so much good for them, already. They neither one had as yet the faintest notion, though, of what it would all turn out to mean, or what sacrifices would be required before they could rightly perceive the nature of their own destinies, the nature of the world around them, even, the world that they perceived with their senses, and above all the nature of the world within, that true yet obscured world, the mysteries of the psyche in all of its true splendor were yet to be revealed to them, or to be wholly embodied by their dual being.

The old one, meditating alone, all at once understood the significance, and perceived the true worth, of the two young souls now making their way towards his place in the mountains, his high dwelling, naturally cut from the rock, and this caused him to shake his head gently while smiling easily to himself. He perceived, too, the nature of the objects that the two carried with them, and what they signified, what was their worth. He realized also that neither the young man nor the young lady as yet understood the depths of fortune that they were the heirs to, nor its gravity.

In days to come Metaxaeus and Akasha would discover together that her dream had been a reliable one: indeed, they would find themselves spending several cycles of seasons lodged in the mountains at the high dwelling of this old sage, as they each learned from him there the several secrets of his ancient spiritual lineage, which were all in due time freely bestowed, and that had themselves been both preserved and passed on from time immemorial.

Their stay in that dwelling of the old hermit was long, beneficent, enlightening, joyful, arduous and soul-altering, and ultimately of the substance of the truth, the truth that was to manifest in the later days of their lives and on through the last pages of the present story.

BOOK XV
The Wheel of the Stars

In our story, it is many years later. A man stands on the beach alone at twilight. It is yet early spring, and there are light flakes of snow falling gently from the sky above, with the small curve of a new moon in one corner of the night sky. It is in that direction, off into the distance and away out from under the clouds that can be seen the first evening stars, their glimmering light just visible in front of a backdrop of deep blue. The old man looks up at this firmament overhead, wonders for a moment about the Great Spirit and some of the things that he has known and seen, now looks askance and checks a different kind of distance, in this the lengthening day's last light. He looks along down the beach and the long line of the shore, for approaching him now out of a watery distance is a figure that may be just a mirage, but really is the one he has been waiting for, for many years, and only now, as she comes closer, can she be seen to be an old woman: her silvering hair flows fully down the slope of her shoulders and comes to rest elegantly in the small of her back. At first the two old lovers recognize each other only as silhouetted forms. But as she draws near to him, her whole shape materializes, she to him, he to her, and it becomes clear that she wears about the mouth her old stoic expression, and that only the corners of her eyes seem to give something hidden away, whilst her eyes themselves are dancingly the brightest thing on that beach, emanating from them a light more luminous than either the silver new moon or the emergent distant stars. In her dark hair are flecks of the fallen snow. She clasps him by the hand finally and evidently has nothing to say: he looks deep and long into those soft and mesmerizing, melting, wondering, mercurial brown eyes, searching their bright light, and only then, in that moment, does he at last realize that he is prepared, and answers their light from the fire that burns in his own bright-dark eyes, and together these two begin to rise and vanish, into the bright-dark vault overhead, slowly upwards into the primeval dusk. As the snow continues to descend whitely along the line of the beach, the waves to curl and recede, the stars lastingly bright, and the new moon the usherer into new space, new worlds. Seek them now in the winds, and in the seasons, the summers and autumns, the long rivers and the rippling brooks, the tidal patterns, the ancient trees, the rhythms of our oceans, and the night sky. Their constellation has been thrown into the wheel of the stars, that smile eternally down, from beyond the roof of the world.

BOOK XVI
Not a Word to Say

It is now several years earlier again: two people meet one another for the first time in a long time. Their greeting is warm, but the look in their eyes is vague. They have been away from one another for too long, and cannot reach the words that would say what they would say to each other. Their love for each other remains the fire of their now separate lives, but still the words will not come. Awkwardly they part again, having been borne together only briefly, and with only the long train of memories to tide them over through all the long desolation of time spent apart one from the other. Who knew, they ask themselves, that love could lead to such torment?

BOOK XVII
Riddled Hearts

The spirit works mightily in the world (where time is no barrier to it at all,) and yet more mightily, perhaps, in the ever invisible soul. Yet it takes the greatest of faiths, when all faith is a form of constancy, a kind of illimitable patience. Indeed, there is a burning arc pressed deep into the heart of human beings, aflame there and awaiting a realization that will reveal to women and men the removal of all boundaries, and the final annihilation of all obstructions. Such is the nature of our being-in-the-world: we live and move and have our being in a transmaterial universe, but think and act and even will as though we were somehow bound in the dim. The infinite vast of possibility which oft lies on just the other side of a bad outlook, merely, is to our mindsight nearly always undetectable, and thus out of reach.

They never quarreled: they only knew, beyond a certain point, and in the same difficult but wondrous way that they had always known everything which had led them to each other in the first place, that they must for a long season be parted from each other. He made his living for many years in the city by the sea, but day by day his heart was filled only with her. She in turn returned to her parent's home and made her own livelihood by writing down some of what had long been her favorite stories to tell to children: Akasha was the author of children's books, and in the city by the sea Metaxaeus had not been taught to read, but was nevertheless the collector of each bound and colorfully illustrated volume that she had ever produced. They lived that way, separately, for many, many years, and Metaxaeus never did see again either his parents or the village of his boyhood. Had he only known, on that day so long ago when he had set out early in the morning after his practice by the old well, that he would never return. Akasha, though, at his request, had upon a time kindly inked a letter to his mother and father letting them know all that could be said about his life abroad and his work and his love for the girl, yea their love for each other.

But what, then, was the source of their pains, and of their separation? And what all had come to pass during the cycles of seasons spent in the mountains whilst each were still in their early youth? What were the reasons of the spirit? What were its ultimate designs for these two hearts of gold? And what had all of the intervening days to do with their meeting on that long dark beach?

BOOK XVIII
Spirit of the Earth

The day they arrived in the mountains was one of blistering cold: the light of the noonday sun was blinding coming off the abundant snows, but seemed to give off no heat whatsoever. And the winds only made it worse, as they swept stingingly down the narrow channel between immense ridgelines only to whip malevolently at the small uncovered patches of bare skin on our two travelers. They, again, had no idea where they were heading, and in a kind of stark confusion only turned this way and that baffled as to what even to look out for. Fortunately, before long they spotted a large bird with strange markings on its beak and tail-feathers, that seemed to be circling towards a particular place not far from where they stood bewildered: with only the presence of this strange bird to go by, then, they resolved to scale the height to the precise place where the bird was forming circles in the sky.

The last part of their climb proved to be the most arduous of all, but thankfully it led them to the opening of a small fissure in the side of the mountain. They gratefully made their way into the rock cavern, and out of the gales now howling beyond the entrance, only to discover that although it was clearly a comfortable dwelling, nobody was presently at home there in that mountainous cave. Yet after having come so far, they were neither one bashful about having a look around: and they soon discovered that the cave was very spacious, and had two separate tunnels, each wide and high, that ran off from the main entrance and culminated in large cavernous rooms more back towards the heart of the great mountain. Confident of their location, they settled in and made themselves at home, even starting a small fire from which they received much welcome warmth. Soon, they felt certain, they would meet and know the old one whom Akasha had seen in her dream. Now that they were cozy and warm, they were filled with anticipation for their introduction to this strange old hermit of the mountains.

It was sometime in the night that they heard a strange noise: long since asleep on the floor of the cave, they each rose quickly and stoked the fire that had died down in the night, whilst Metaxaeus with a flaming brand gathered up from the fire stepped cautiously out from the cave entrance to see if he could confront whatever it was that had been the cause of the strange sound which had woken both he and Akasha from their sound sleep. There was a smell of embers on the wind. Overhead, he thought he could just make out the circling motion of what he supposed must be the same strange bird, with the peculiar tail markings, that had led them to the place where they now were, earlier that day. Just in that moment, while Metaxaeus was still straining his eyes to perceive the silhouette of the circling bird against the dark sky, there began to issue a soft light from one of the tunnels of the cavern now set behind Akasha and Metaxaeus, so that they abandoned their investigation of the bird circling overhead and went to see what was the source of this gentle light now emanating from one of the tunnels in the cave where they had been sleeping so peacefully only moments before.

It was at the rear of the rightward tunnel, then, that they discovered the source of the softly emanating light: the old one himself was indeed at home, and must have entered without disturbing them sometime earlier in the evening, but was now sitting alone and peacefully in an upright posture of deep meditation. Immersed in a kind of trance, with light pouring from his body. Stealthily Metaxaeus and Akasha made their way back out of the room and once again into the central entrance area and settled themselves back down to sleep, with a deep feeling of peace now enveloping them as they drifted quietly and warmly off to unconsciousness.

Akasha that same night dreamt (once again) of the old sage seated reposefully there in the room of the cavern, and her heart was somehow infused with a strong sense of certainty that she and Metaxaeus had made the right decision in traveling here to learn from this man whose body had already been witnessed to be a living source of light. Whilst Metaxaeus, for his part, also felt filled with the pleasant assurance that despite all of the twists and turns that his own life had taken over the past half year or so, that he now found himself nonetheless certainly in the right place, and that he had not at any time really gone off course. He felt that all was just as it should be: first his fateful meeting with Akasha, and now their being here together at this high mountain dwelling. Absentmindedly in his sleeping, he moved closer to Akasha and curled himself gently around the feel of her body, physically drinking in the sense of her warmth and the rhythm of her breathing: he knew in his core that he would be alright and more than alright, indescribably happy, so long as he could only be wherever she was, and then she moved one of her hands to rest easily upon the side of his body and they slept like that, as it were now dreaming together.

Daylight made its way into the entrance of the cave at an early hour, as they were situated along the eastern slope of the great mountain. Akasha and Metaxaeus awoke to the sound of an already crackling fire, and found themselves to be once again grateful this time to find a warm breakfast awaiting them suspended over the flames. Again this old one whose place they had invaded without an introduction was not at home, but they took this warm blaze and ready-made breakfast as an indication of their welcome. Yet they wondered, however, when they would begin to converse with the teacher whom they had so fearlessly sought out up here in the cold snows high above the long valley floor and the timelessly winding course of the great river far below.

Later that same day, before they could feel any claustrophobia from the small space begin to set in, and as the day wore on towards evening, with the first faint tinges of orange emergent over the silhouetted mountain peaks and the gentle lengthening of the one great shadow of the great mountain over the valley floor below, the old sage at last made his appearance at the mouth of the cave and stood there for a moment adorned in nothing more than a rustic red robe and a pair of hide sandals to cover his bare feet. He carried with him a lantern in one hand and the strange bird from the day before was perched upon his other arm wearing a small leathern helmet like those used in falconry. His first words to them were to do with the bird, "This is my companion; you may call her Maya." Then he once again turned away from them and with a quick jerking motion of his arm and a sharp "Tut!" sound he loosed her, as she then rose up swiftly and on strong, large pinions went arcing out of sight beyond the mouth of the cavern.

The old one then stood there silently for several moments, all the while facing away from them and looking out of the cavern's entrance as though watching the trailing flight of the bird as she wound away over the distant mountain peaks. He wore a long white beard and had long white flowing hair and his temples were garnished with white curling locks and at last he turned his presence towards Metaxaeus and Akasha and bid them hello. He smiled broadly, uninhibitedly, and took up a kind of benched seat just above the cavern floor on which he immediately locked himself into a cross-legged position and for the first time and without any other ado of introductions began to make conversation.

"Tell me the truth, what do you think of my home?"

As the winters would pass into spring, and the spring would pass into summer, and the beard of Metaxaeus would continue to lengthen, there would nevertheless be up in this high country no real respite from the snows. There only ever prevailed a white fastness extending over the high mountains as far as the eye could see: stone, desolate, treeless, and magnificent. Only the colors on the valley floor far below would change with the continual passing of one season on into the next, and the temperature where they dwelt would either warm or cool itself slightly and the winds in the summer would mostly abate.

Because of the altitude and because of the cold, then, almost never would the rain fall anywhere upon the high mountain chain, least of all upon the slopes of the great mountain. There was one day, however, that remained in the memories of both Metaxaeus and Akasha, one day of downpour so violent that, looking out from the entrance to the old master's cave, one could see nothing but the drops of water, like ten thousand heavy globules of mercury, spiraling down from the overspreading sky's dark factory, like some cloudworked furnace attempting to quench its own seething and molten core with a superabundant array of waters, with the evergreen Earth gentle and placid beneath a colorful fire of sky in the distance, divinity's rainbow smiling down on a vast dark land. This was their watch, one day, from the height of the great mountain, and each were carried away into such reverie that the violence of the storm, its power and its pageantry, caused to arise in their hearts, suddenly full to bursting, the thought of their families and their friends, and of their teeming lives now so distant from their own, as though the whole vast and lonely world was spread out before them on that deep valley floor. For some inexplicable reason, the often unspeakable, and the almost unrealizable preciousness of all life entered into their hearts in that moment like a flaming brand, like a blue consuming fire suddenly lodged there, irremovably and more than they could stand. So powerful that day was the melancholy of the rain, itself like a force of nature, and one plunging its way steeply into their hearts with an irresistible dominion. Silently Akasha held out her hand, until facing each other sorrowfully yet still full of life and warmth, he kissed her tenderly upon her forehead and then they turned once more to gaze wonderingly out at the rainfall infinity beyond the cavern walls, and straight into the heart of the radiant day itself, this one day radiant in memory and in spirit, a day emanated from the ether of time, and from the one and only Dream of the Great Spirit, onrushingly wreathed in the cloudlets of mind.

Turningly then they wondered. What does it all mean?

Not too distant, from what must have been the very heart of the high mountains, and nestled in the white stones, was a small circle of springs, so that often in the deep submerging twilight, that would nightly descend upon the tall summits, Akasha and Metaxaeus would immerse themselves and lay still awhile, gazing upwards and beaming, at the rich firmament overhead, the spread-out and spiral arms, incandescing in the night sky. At ease beneath the several silent suns, and withal the incalculable quiet of the breath, which would then gently begin to move, to cycle and to pulse, oceanly into the stars, until a moment of remembrance, an instant of recognition which spoke of how love only, had once upon a time affixed this place and all others, created the starshine, the turning of the years and the river's way below.

Awhile later and leaving this place, Akasha's eyes alighted upon a lone white lotus flower, floating upon the surface of a smaller pool nearby, and with no earthly reason for flourishing thus deep in these mountains, which had not wilted from the warmth of the springs. As a sign of something, she decided to keep it, floating alone inside a crystal jar.

The old sage never once made mention of his true name or of anything at all to do with his personal history; and neither did he ever make any inquiry into the two small objects that Metaxaeus and Akasha yet carried with them.

What was the peculiar destiny, then, and for the two of them, of the sculpture of the phoenix and the lotus blossom that Metaxaeus carried with him or of the amulet that Akasha preserved on her person? Why had these two strange artifacts such a deep-seated inner connection to the souls of their owners?

The last lesson of the old one, which was a metamorphosis into the consort of Maya, first crystallizing into heat and ash and then rising up into the air, seemed to intimate that he had no intention of answering any more questions. The years spent in the mountains were now finished, and lining the cavern walls had been many strange volumes: books of prophecy with their elaborate symbolisms, and their brightly opalescent illuminations, but these had held between their antique bindings only the barest intimations of what was apparently possible in actuality. The old one and his consort were shamans, and totems, and true spirits of the Earth.

And so the question became, What kind of a world was this? In any event, and after this the final epiphany of the old one's true identity, it was clear that Akasha and Metaxaeus were from here supposed to make their own way.

BOOK XIX
The Word

"Immortality," became the word that he would whisper to her....

Years later, she would notice it again in the voice of the winds, or the sound of the crashing waves, or discover it in the notes of birdsong whilst alone in the wood near the home of her family, her childhood home.

She began to feel that it was the sole and essential intimation of all of the songs which she had been taught to sing as a child. One day she found a new book in her town's library that was about the OmniSoul, also called the Soul of the World, and in its pages there was expressed absolutely no doubt about the immemorial validity, and the reality, of this one idea, cherished by lovers and longed for, ultimately in one instance or another, by all.

And it had been his word: he would whisper it to her as he had whispered to her her own name on the day that they had met, or even in the same way that she had caught his name on the wind, somehow, on that other day, so long ago, before they had even ever seen each other.

Like a sunrise over the eastern mountains, this word now had to it an ascendancy over her mind: it had entered, ever so gradually, into the forefront of her thoughts about her life and the future that it held. Like the way that the world would glow in that morning light, cusped as it were over the lonely rolling hills, Akasha would stand in the glory of that one thought, that one ruling idea of again being together with him, and that on and on not as though forever, but rather as forever really and truly.

Her faith, in this idea, was the reason she was without fear.

And it kept her alive.

Like a river that meets the sea, she would enter at last into those shining waters. She would become the scented pines; the buzzing of insects; the steam rising up from the Earth early in the morning just before dawn. Her long quest was very nearly finished: soon she would be one with the spirit: and she would live forever. She believed it in her heart.

BOOK XX
Approaching the End

God's painterly cloudworks; the arc of the horizon; and at night the atmospheric stars' long look down the sidereal scope of infinity....

What shall you wonder about, when you have grown old?

Unfold one story.
For the Universe,
It is said,
To be captured,
Must only ever be retold.

BOOK XXI
Unraveling the Threads

The scope of allowed time, spiritually considered, is nothing short of aeonian. And yet, all things would seem to sooner or later elapse: the preciousness of love or the life of a star, even. One day gone. As the Great Spirit oversees the centuries, so Death would seem to have total dominion.

Hence the importance, the secret, finally, of transformation: of a continual transformation as renewal. As an inlet for the understanding into the invisible. Like mirrors in the clouds, or thunder that is summoned by the force of the lightning, or the lightning itself that in its flashing will destroy an oak tree in a way not very different than the moisture from underground will split the acorn. Then, after some time, the invisible emergence, and activity, of the sap, of lifeblood in the veins. Singingly within, we aspire; and become eventually only that that we always already were. This is what was communicated by the touch of the magus when Akasha was a girl, and what was conveyed in its essence in the tutelage of Metaxaeus, at only a little later age, by the sagely old woman, ancient bird and the old master's lover and twin, who in this story has called herself by the name of Maya.

There was a disappearance and a shattering: twin instances that begat a return to the old forge this time with new knowledge and a new aim.

Metaxaeus' riverguide once upon a time, had winked down at him while piloting their small skiff down the long current of the great river, because he had glimpsed for a moment the artistry, the ingenuity, and the brilliance of

Metaxaeus' work in stone, but he had winked also because he knew the sage of the great mountain and he knew Maya and he even knew, from Metaxaeus' own thoughts, of the girl, the young woman Akasha. Metaxaeus' riverguide had himself, in only one of what now seemed like a chain of former lives, been the reputed blacksmith-healer of a small village nondescript and not too far away from the old river whose course they had then traveled.

Whilst he realized in himself that he never would possess or for that matter really even understand the powers of either "Maya" or the agreeable sage, and while he knew deep down that his own life was to be a more solitary lot (only, perhaps, for another cycle or two...), still he knew, also, that his powers were in their own right greater than any and so it was that he had, once upon a time, been the fashioner of Akasha's now shattered and endarkened amulet as well as of another small sculpture that he had at one time, many years ago, passed along to a girl so young that how could she really be the teller of such tales? Deeply now he sighed while finishing his work.

In order to recapture the light, he will need the presence of the girl (the lady) and in order to remake the bird and the flower anew there was now only one who could do so. He would require the handiwork of Metaxaeus the man in the city by the sea, the masterworker in stone, now living and working along the coast was this man who could fashion the very breakers or the ebbing and flowing and planetary surf into rock or marble or stone. And not least, of course, there was an indubitable remarkability to the statue of a woman whom he had carved, a few years ago, and which was now dedicated and stood proudly (full of grace,) and unbelievably alive and erect and supple and tall and strong and wise there in the plaza and town center of the proud ancient city by the sea and which had etched into its plinth, 'To our most eminent giver of gifts, and our city's only adopted daughter, the Storyteller by the River, we give you the name, too, of our Storyteller by the Sea. May your words keep us ever young at heart.'

Now, however, at an hour so urgent, how would he summon them without light, without time, and without the help of the river? Reflecting for a moment, he recalled an old bird-whistle that someone wise had once taught him as a child, growing up far, far away. So he began softly to rise in that song; he knew that it would be his last act, before overturning one more time the world.

BOOK XXII
Akasha is Summoned

"Never mind that people might transform themselves into birds, or vice versa: because a story is, in the end, just a story, and only needs to find a way to live forever. The drift is immortality, only, and that first and last. Where a good-bye can last forever, or a simple shadow can be the illuminator of countless minds. Where the last song of a passing poet might translate itself into the heartshine of a dying person worlds away. It is only a story: and yet everybody knows this already. Everybody realizes these things. So let us make the world in a day."

Akasha had spoken these words once, and she now remembered, being at the time not yet the age of her fellows to whom she had been speaking, and they were hardly twelve. Reflecting now, she recognized, of course, that she had not really intended such wisdom, and had understood very little, really, of what she had then said. Yet she realized also, and now with the wisdom of many years, that she had mistaken only one thing.

That a story was not, always, just a story: for if such things as she had seen could really happen, and could take place in the world, then what was the world, after all? And if the Maker of the World had brought this world at one time into being, as surely (she felt) had been done, and if a person such as herself were to discover the same substance, or the same spirit, as it were, with which that original illuminative feat had been performed, then why could not she be the heavenly artificer working with the same materials, the world, a story, remade in her own words and therefore wrought finally of the same stuff of which the Great Spirit had once upon a time wrought us, the stuff of the soul? Could one who knew of the spirit, who was herself at one with the spirit, who lived and breathed and moved and had her being in that spirit, the arch-mystery and the arch-triumph of existence, herself create a change in the world, in the cosmos, by entering into other people's hearts, and affecting a difference there? She believed beyond all doubt not only that she could do such a thing, but that such a thing had indeed been done already in countless songs that were sung, or in epic stories that were told, or poems that were written, pictures made, or aetherically sculpted stone.

Coaxed into range, alight in the evening, and out beyond the flash of the fireflies that she busied herself with penciling in for one of her books that she was creating, was the sudden shape of an old friend.

'And what news have you brought here to my home in the woods, old friend?'

BOOK XXIII
Metaxaeus is Called

Electric blue dragonflies alighted, like small omens, playfully, dazzlingly, along a dusty outdoor workbench, as though just materialized from the very freshets of spring. For it was indeed the season of renewal, albeit each one had been chiseled from stone, and were now resting beside levitating hummingbirds, graceful lakeswans, blossoming bluebells, and unimaginable bodies.

The entrance to Metaxaeus' garden workshop was an ornate wooden arbor with the one word 'Eternity' carved into the woodwork. It was an inscription that left no doubt as to Metaxaeus' artistic philosophy, or his feelings about the durability of his chosen medium. But his stonework was a paradox: by his art he could commonly transform marble or rock into an almost astral substance. His sculptures were like shape-shifters every one, and threatened to change their form at even the slightest upwelling of dust.

As a matter of fact, the winds that would periodically blow in off the ocean were enough to induce in his men and his women, his creatures, objects, a kind of living trance, all of course standing perfectly still in the midst of their beatific surroundings; they had nonetheless quite enough magnetism roiling and blooming within their bodies and limbs as if to sustain a beating heart.

He had only to glance up from his labors in order to understand who it was was there. "Old friend," he said, "What brings you here and so suddenly to this place of inward disquiet, though my heart rejoices to see you?"

"Quickly: and prepare yourself for a meeting with Akasha."

BOOK XXIV
The Remaking

Creativity and grace are the hallmarks of spirit. Co-ultimates in the quest for love. Does the Great Spirit answer prayers?

Dark locket: lightless, dormant, vulnerable....

Light that must have simply faded out through the years, and once altogether gone, left the thing pervious, the small object breakable. She dropped it only once, darkly, and the pieces, the splinters, were as illimitable as the stars. She had all her life disliked the shedding of tears, but now her grief was torrential. Why had the light gone out? And how was it possible to lose such a thing? She felt disfigured, undone, dead. There was nobody to whom to turn, and that aloneness of hers was all the more unforgiveable for its majesty....

His was at the bottom of the sea. He had always known that what he should have done was to have given it to her on the day that they had met. Now, since she was the sea, he felt that he had only returned it to its home. Never once did he either rue or regret the years. He loved her so much.

He loved her too mightily....

They arrived at the mystical site simultaneously.

Wood dark and muddy, yet place of fire, place of light.

There was a man standing there already thrusting a crucible into the heart of the forge, oblivious of anything besides the small chamber of molten gold.

They could not look each other in the eye.

"Come forth." Was the command. He did so immediately, unhesitatingly, realizing that everything was in the balance....

The metal cooled quickly, but for some precious moments remained malleable. Soon there would be a shape of unreceding fulfillment, a miniature blossom with enough power in it for it to become the restorator of everything that had been lost.

Consequently he worked quickly, almost too quickly, sensing the moment, understanding the urgency, and trying to fashion a remedy.

What she was asked to pass through was the true fire, rebirth and the sibling of death. One last trial of spirit: a process dark and final. Sublime magic. Inchoate light.

The first stage of the remaking was complete: a small 24 karat lotus the likes of which....

Then Akasha was led away; the trouble with tears was that they always gave something away, but in this they were exactly what was counted on, and would be precisely what was needed, tiny spheroidal prisms via which only the most ancient magic could be coerced into yielding its dominion....

Metaxaeus began to prise from the rock the next multi-karated gemstone: its jagged surface to be transformed, in minutes, into a blue fire, a flashing and resurrected phoenix.

But also there was to be something else, this time a more ensuing species of light....

Her heart was breaking: the feeling which she kept inside her was being made to force its way through her bodily being as though each and every pore were being coerced into a releasement of its inmost essence. Yet never had she felt so close to the understanding of what it must be like to be an explosive and newborn star. The cells of her body ignited into a physical core that she had never even dreamt existed: it was as if the teeming quintillions of atoms that constituted her body were descending in a starshine or otherwise furious heat so maddening to the threshold of her psyche that somewhere in a kind of fixed infinity, an interstellar space within, she only witnessed herself wondering if she could powerfully outlive the only reason for such unwonted suffering, such inimitable splendor, this unearthed incorruptible mettle in her soul, an explosion of white light, and the sovereign resuscitation of an at last invincible love.

She had to catch her breath: the whole earth was still turning inside a lost moment, within the perfect evaporation of time and the finally supreme exhalation of all light....

She had not known—how could she have been expected to realize?—that he had been standing right there, right beside her the whole time, and had caught the entire metamorphosis, the full emanation of unwilling ultimate light. They had, with the help and with the summons of the original magus and their two old friends, captured and fused and re-sculpted the old disintegrated artifacts; now gold and sapphire and light within light, this newly forged adamantine structure as solemn and living proof of willpower and love and an ultimately triumphant spiritual grace.

The moment for miracles arced into passing. The clime of awareness without an other, without a second, is as dismal a gray blanket as the solar gold-and-blue sunfire is the light of this our only world, or as the vast canopy of the stars is our only cosmic architecture.

Each of them living alone again, though now whole, restored, and recognizing that their time still had not come, they each set about that which they loved most to do, he sculpting in stone in the splendorous city by the sea, and she weaving her stories and living peacefully in the home of her childhood, her lifelong home along the shores of the river.

She kept the new thing in her possession; but the only name that she could think to give it was Spirit. Periodically, she would gaze into it, and it would glow up at her so fiercely that she wondered what all that entrapped blue fire, that light beyond light, would one day accomplish for new and different lovers.

One day, she advanced to the edge of the great river, and stood there languidly along its banks beginning to gaze, almost longingly, into the approach of the oncoming storm, the vast seasonal rains and their dark thunderheads. Up there in a final sky, the amazing halo of the endistanced sun, for one last, lingering and fiery moment shone its light through the dark embankment of the falling rain, and the gentle but thunderous rainfall infinity....

She thought for a moment of his word to her, "immortality," and how she knew it had come true. And knowing that their time would soon be here, she set the lighted object in the mud along the riverbank, not much differently at all, really, than as had been done on a similar day long ago. She smiled a little. She had outgrown in a moment her old stoical dislike for the shedding of tears, and now cried easily, appreciatively as she took one last long look above at the darkly shining sky, that final and furious sun, and behind and above it, the eternal wheel of the stars....

When the spring would arrive, she would know then that it was their time, and she would be on her way again, this time with no return home, but only that final, skyborne departure into the heart of things, and into the heart of all, into the heart of each other, on that twilit beach, their dusky song, risen forever and gone.

Spirited away.

EPILOGUE
The Sapphire Song

Furrowed pages blow dustily along the floor of an abandoned workshop. Notebooks, filled with stories and sketches, and brimming with characters and events magnificent, are stacked totteringly up along the walls.

In the small courtyard stand sculptures of men and women, flowers, animals, and trees. Breathingly the winds descend upon the myriad moments, the shapes and the forms and the stories, the dusty pages and the standing statues.

Blindingly comes in a flash of white, and all is enshadowed for a moment. Liltingly then the bee stings: a sparrow takes flight: and the spirit, as ever, has done its work. So livingly, breathingly, we turn upon each other, but now only in order to love. To love in the spirit, as in the blue crystalline light, of a fluid and Sapphire Song.

Made in the USA
Monee, IL
02 October 2021

465352b5-1b1a-4b97-8ffb-315a87ebb198R01